FIRESTORMERS

Firestormers is published by
Stone Arch Books,
a Capstone imprint
1710 Roe Crest Drive
North Mankato, Minnesota 56003
www.mycapstone.com

Cataloging-in-Publication Data is available on the
Library of Congress website.
ISBN: 978-1-4965-3308-1 (library binding)
ISBN: 978-1-4965-3312-8 (eBook)

Summary:
As the son of a state senator, Lieutenant Jason Garrett
had most of his life handed to him on a silver platter. His
father even pulled a few strings to secure him a top spot
on the world's newest, most elite wildfire fighting crew:
FIRESTORMERS. But standing on front lines against
hundred-foot walls of 2,000-degree flames, Garrett must
rely on his own courage, heart, and crewmates to survive.

Printed and bound in Canada.
009638F16

FIRESTORMERS
FIRE FRONT

written by CARL BOWEN
cover illustration by MARC LEE

STONE ARCH BOOKS
a capstone imprint

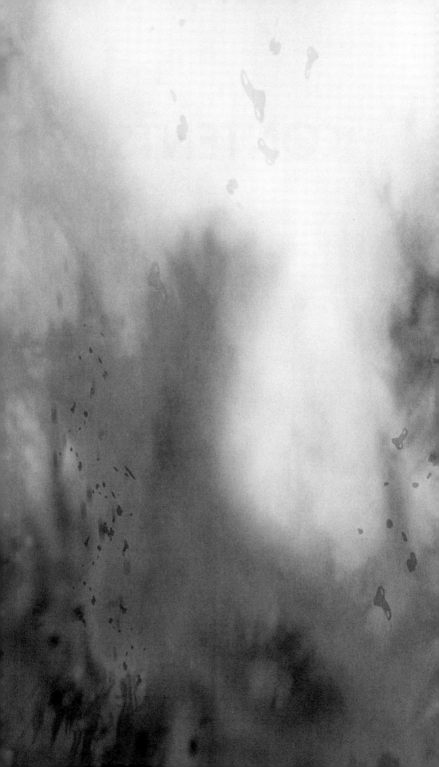

CONTENTS

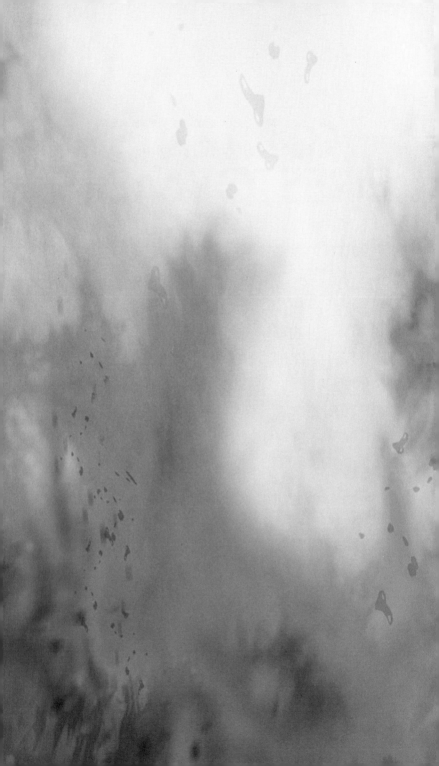

FIRESTORMERS
Elite Firefighting Crew

As the climate changes and the population grows, wildland fires increase in number, size, and severity. Only an elite group of men and women are equipped to take on these immense infernos. Like the toughest military units, they have the courage, the heart, and the technology to stand on the front lines against hundred-foot walls of 2,000-degree flames. They are the FIRESTORMERS.

KLAMATH NATIONAL FOREST

Established:

May 6, 1905

Coordinates:

41°30′01″ N

123°20′00″ W

Location:

California, USA

Oregon, USA

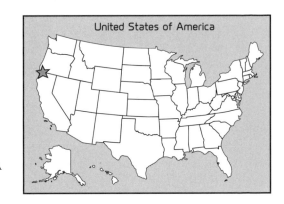

United States of America

Size:

1,737,774 acres (2,715 square miles)

Elevation Range:

450–8,900 feet above sea level

Ecology:

Stretching from northern California into southern Oregon, Klamath National Forest is a rich, diverse biosphere. Stands of old-growth ponderosa pine and Douglas fir dominate the landscape from the banks of the Salmon and Scott Rivers to the top of the Klamath Mountains. Many threatened and endangered species call this region home, including northern spotted owls and wild coho salmon.

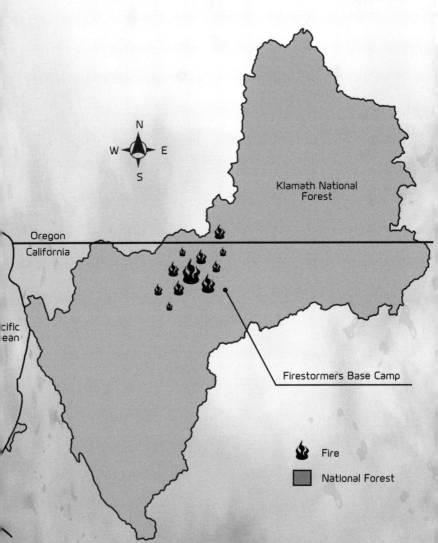

Klamath National Forest

Oregon
California

Pacific Ocean

Firestormers Base Camp

Fire

National Forest

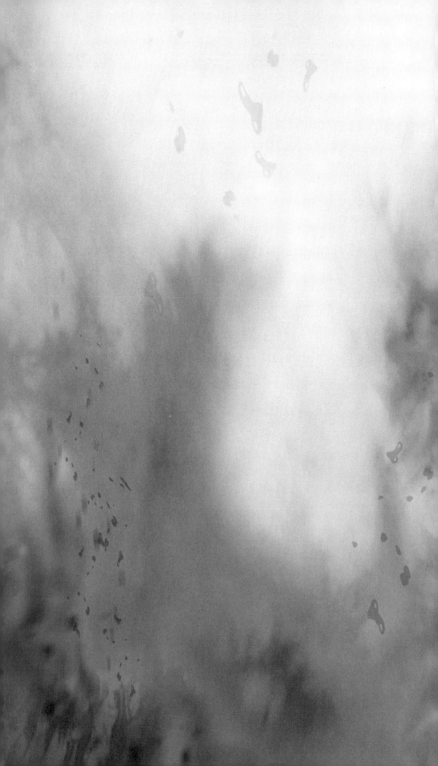

CHAPTER ONE

Lieutenant Jason Garrett didn't consider himself a thrill seeker. He didn't consider himself a hero or even much of a leader. How then, he wondered, did he wind up inside a CASA 212 turboprop, ready to jump onto the fire front of a thousand-degree inferno? It was enough to make him question his sanity.

Or maybe, he thought, *I'm just a closet adrenaline junkie.*

"Five minutes!" shouted the flight's jumpmaster as he worked his way through the plane's cramped passenger compartment.

The jumpmaster was a kid just out of college, who'd been hurling himself out of airplanes for a decade already. Lieutenant Garrett had it on good authority that the kid was the best in California. Still, Garrett would've preferred that someone older than himself perform the final checks on his crew's chutes and gear riggings.

Lieutenant Garrett would've also preferred to be on the ground, all things considered.

He knew how to skydive — he'd been on dozens of training jumps — but this was his first jump as an official smokejumper. It was also his first mission as strike team leader for the nation's newest, most elite firefighting crew: Firestormers.

That fact alone should have made Jason Garrett proud.

It didn't. The lieutenant's training should have overridden his nervousness.

It hadn't.

As the plane neared its designated drop zone, Lieutenant Garrett couldn't help but wonder, *What the heck am I doing here?*

* * *

"Dad, what am I doing here?" Garrett had asked his father three months earlier.

Jason's father, Senator John "Big Jack" Garrett, had invited him to breakfast out of the blue. After working back-to-back, twenty-four-hour shifts at the Portland fire station, Jason would've preferred to sleep in.

But nobody said no to Big Jack.

"I talked to the governor yesterday," Big Jack said through a mouthful of thick-cut bacon. "He tells me you turned down a medal for what you did last week."

"You mean my job?" Jason asked. He

hadn't eaten much of his own breakfast, which his father had ordered for him like he was a kid. "I don't want a medal for doing my job."

Big Jack slurped a forkful of sunny-side-up eggs. "You saved eighteen people's lives, son. Kids, even. Heck, you should be fighting off interviews from CNN, Fox News, or even *Good Morning America*."

"It's just the job, Dad," Jason insisted. "Some days are better than others."

"Bah, you deserve it," Big Jack asserted. He looked around at the other restaurant patrons and announced, "This guy's a hero! And he's my son!"

Jason tried to sink into the diner's greasy tile floor.

The day his father was boasting about had been a good one, no doubt. Jason's station had received a call about a fire at Portland's largest high school. Most of the students and faculty had made it out just fine, but a faulty alarm in the school's theater had failed to alert the drama club. Jason led a firefighting crew through the blaze and smoke to set the trapped students and faculty free.

Minutes afterward, dozens of videos of him helping the drama teacher limp to safety, surrounded by coughing, sweating student actors, surfaced on the Internet. The fact that the high schoolers were dressed for a production of *Cats* helped the video go viral overnight. The local news interviewed Jason — twice. Calls praising Jason's heroic act flooded the fire chief's office. The mayor even congratulated him personally.

"Let me ask you," Big Jack went on, picking up his sourdough toast and gesturing with it as he spoke. "Have you changed your mind about campaigning for me next year?"

Big Jack had been asking this whenever he was up for reelection for as long as Jason had been a firefighter. Jason always told him the same thing.

"You'll do just fine without me, Dad."

"Thought so," the senator said. "And since that's what I figured you'd say, let's talk about why I really wanted to meet you. How much do you know about the Forest Service?"

Jason blinked a few times, caught slightly off guard. "Not much. It's a federal agency, right?" he replied. "Watches out for National Parks and stuff like that?"

"In a nutshell," his father confirmed. "They're the people most worried about wildland fires. They used to make those Smokey Bear commercials, remember?"

"Who?" Jason asked, looking puzzled.

Big Jack shook his head in disappointment. "Before your time, I guess. Anyway, the

Forest Service has a huge budget for fighting wildfires, but last year they blew through the money just two months into fire season. So they're trying something different this time around. They're calling their new program the National Elite Interagency Wildfire Rapid Response Strike Force."

"That's a mouthful," Jason said. That went for the name as well as for the bite of toast his father insisted on chewing as he said it.

Big Jack burped. "The guy in charge calls them the *Firestormers*. And right now he's recruiting the cream of the crop from fire services all over the West, looking for folks willing to fight these infernos wherever they pop up."

Jason's eyes narrowed. "And . . ."

"I submitted your name."

"What?" Jason exclaimed. "I don't know anything about fighting wildland fires.

They're completely different from structure fires. I'm not trained for —"

"Relax, kiddo," Big Jack said. "They'll train you. Besides, it's just digging ditches, basically. It's hardly complicated."

Jason doubted that.

"The real work's done at the organizational level," Big Jack continued. "The folks who coordinate all the ditch digging and the bulldozing and whatnot — they're mostly the ones doing the heavy lifting. It takes a keen mind, strong organizational skills, and leadership abilities. Everybody from your station's lieutenant all the way up to the governor's office agrees you've got all that in spades."

"Maybe because you told them to think that," Jason mumbled.

Big Jack shrugged, though he couldn't hide a wry smile. "Folks listen when I talk sense," the senator said, quoting his favorite campaign slogan. "And now I want you to listen. The Forest Service has appointed an old veteran fire chief out of California, Anna MacElreath, to head up this strike force. She's meeting with fire chiefs and local authorities in at-risk wildland areas. She's going to be here in Portland next week, and I want you to meet with her."

"Why?"

"Well, for one thing, as far as the family business goes, this is some great leadership experience," Big Jack explained.

"Family business? You mean politics?" Jason asked. "Pass."

"Not politics," Big Jack said, though that was clearly what he meant. "Community service. Besides, this is going to fast-track that promotion to lieutenant you've been waiting for. Also, you'd be a federal employee instead of a county firefighter. Better pay, better benefits, better union representation. Probably better equipment. And you'd get to travel regularly — at least from Arizona to Alaska."

Jason said nothing.

Big Jack stood, pulled a wad of cash from his back pocket, and threw half of it on his empty breakfast plate. "All I'm saying is this is good work that we all know you're capable of, Jason. Just meet with this chief, all right? Talk to her. See if the Firestormers are something you'd be interested in. I wouldn't want you to miss the opportunity, in case it turns out to be just right for you."

Jason sighed. "Okay, Dad," he finally answered. "I'll talk to her."

"Attaboy!"

* * *

"We're over the drop zone, Lieutenant," the jumpmaster declared. He popped the seal on the turboprop's door and slid it open. Wind roared into the passenger compartment, silencing the Firestormers crew.

Lieutenant Garrett stood from his jump seat and walked toward the open door of the CASA-212. Five thousand feet below, eleven thousand acres of California's Klamath National Forest burned. Garrett felt the heat quickly warm his face and the smoke sting his eyes.

Nobody says no to Big Jack, Lieutenant Garrett thought.

Then he gave the jumpmaster a thumbs-up and looked back at his team.

Two dozen determined faces stared back at him expectantly. Lieutenant Garrett didn't know if they were waiting for his order, or if they wanted him to say something inspirational to commemorate the first Firestormers mission.

"Who wants to storm a fire?!" Garrett finally shouted over the turboprop's roaring engine. *Ugh,* he groaned to himself at the bad action-hero catchphrase.

Nobody moved or spoke. Big Jack's campaign slogan, "Folks listen when I talk sense," echoed in Garrett's ears, and he couldn't help but chuckle.

Just then, one of his crew bosses — Sergeant Heath Rodgers — stood, reached up, and banged a fist twice against the plane's low ceiling.

"Hoorah!" he called.

Jason smiled and repeated the gesture. "Hoorah!"

As one, each and every Firestormer did the same. Even the jumpmaster did it, grinning from ear to ear.

"Hoorah!" they shouted in unison.

Let's get on with it, thought Lieutenant Garrett, standing at the open door of the CASA-212 turboprop.

Garrett swallowed hard and leaped from the plane. Behind him, twenty-five men and women followed, and together they fell toward the devilish inferno below.

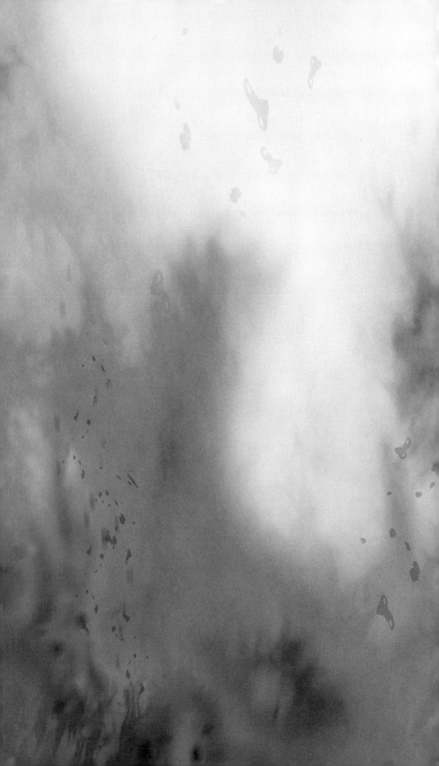

CHAPTER TWO

Growing up in downtown Portland, Jason Garrett had never actually seen a wildland fire up close. His training had given him an idea of the scale and scope of such events, but nothing had prepared him for the inferno's raw power.

Lieutenant Garrett pulled his chute's ripcord and — *FWOOSH!* — the rushing air grew silent, replaced by the hideous roar of the fire below.

Across the horizon, he saw flames eating at the hills like a hungry dragon. White-orange tendrils swirled from the forest's undergrowth to the tops of the tallest trees. Smoke blackened the sky in all directions, piling up into the beginnings of a nearby thunderhead.

Suddenly, Lieutenant Garrett's chute pulled him off course, awakening him from the awe-inspiring scene. He looked around. Other Firestormers struggled with their chutes as well, fighting desperately to steer back toward the drop zone. If his crew landed outside of it, Garrett knew they'd have to struggle uphill before they could get to work. But he didn't want to land too close to the fire either, for obvious reasons.

Convection currents, Lieutenant Garrett thought.

He'd never experienced them firsthand, but he'd read about them in his training manuals.

As the fire burned, it hurled superheated air upward. This rising hot air caused surrounding cooler air to flow inward and take its place, which the fire then heated and pushed upward and away again. This churning cycle of convection stirred intense, unpredictable winds this close to the blaze.

Garrett grabbed the parachute's steering lines and pulled on them like his life depended on it. Because it did.

The lines tore through his Kevlar gloves, but Garrett managed to stabilize his chute.

Soon, he and the other Firestormers were on the ground in Klamath National Park — a mere five hundred yards from the fire front.

Lieutenant Garrett unhooked his chute and gathered it up as quickly as he could. He then made his way to a hilltop while his team pattered down around him.

Garrett stared the fire in its beastly face and tried not to gulp like a cartoon character. Seeing the fire from the sky was one thing; looking at the blaze on its own level was worse. He felt like an ant that fancied itself a dragon slayer.

That, however, was what his training was for.

* * *

Those training weeks had been the most nightmarish, demanding, and rewarding of Lieutenant Garrett's life. Covering topics such as skydiving, primitive survival, geography, meteorology, emergency care, and fire science, the training had expanded his mind and toughened his body faster than he'd thought possible.

His PT stats and technical proficiencies had earned praise from his instructors and impressed Chief MacElreath. He'd even earned the respect of fellow trainees — some of whom had years of wildland experience.

By the end of the training, Garrett was a standout candidate, top of his class. Chief MacElreath had not only assured him a spot on her new strike force, but she'd given him a position as the strike team leader.

The force had one strike team at the moment, consisting of four crews of five people each, plus Garrett and four auxiliary rangers. That Garrett had been given command of that team had not gone over well with everyone, but Chief MacElreath made it clear that she felt Garrett was the best person for the job. The others would just have to swallow whatever misgivings they might have and do the job they'd been hired to do.

Digging his radio out of a belt holster, Garrett keyed it to the plane's frequency and called to the onboard crew.

"Air Ops One, this is Strike One," he said.

"Go ahead, Strike One."

"We're down and secure," Garrett reported. "Ready for cargo."

"Roger that," the pilot replied. "Give us a ping."

Lieutenant Garrett dug a high-tech computer tablet out of his cargo pants, removed his torn gloves, and swiped the touchscreen. A handful of digital icons appeared in a cluster. Garrett tapped the one marked JPADS, and a topographical map of the drop zone appeared on the screen. Markers showed the position of Garrett's strike team and the CASA-212 above.

"Ping," Lieutenant Garrett said over the radio.

"Yeah, we got it, Strike One," the pilot said, making Garrett feel silly for pointing out the obvious. "Cargo's away. Good luck."

"Thanks."

At that, the CASA-212 turboprop's marker banked away on the tablet's screen and markers representing the cargo arced toward the ground.

Lieutenant Garrett glanced up in time to see the actual plane turning away as large bundles dropped out of the back. As the packages fell, red, white, and blue parafoil chutes blossomed above them, slowing their descent.

Lieutenant Garrett turned his attention back to his tablet, considering how best to remotely guide the cargo to where his team could reach it.

The technology that allowed him to do so was called the Joint Precision Airdrop System. It consisted of two systems developed by the Army and the Air Force. The first included satellite-linked weather tracking and global positioning systems that allowed the packages to track their relative position to the impact point.

The second system included decelerator lines on the sides of the parafoils to cause drag. Applied with precision, that drag forced the parafoils to change direction in midair. Working together, the JPADS units could track where the packages were supposed to land and force them back in the right direction if wind blew them astray.

From his tablet, Lieutenant Garrett could have controlled the flight remotely by hand, but he decided to trust the computer to get the job done. That was what it was for, after all.

While waiting for the cargo to touch down, Lieutenant Garrett shrugged out of his rigging and stowed the parachute inside. As he was finishing that, Sergeant Heath Rodgers, one of his four crew bosses, joined him on the hilltop.

Lieutenant Garrett didn't know much about Rodgers, except that he'd been in the Marine Corps before moving back home to Arizona and becoming a firefighter.

Sergeant Rodgers didn't say anything. He seemed to be waiting for Garrett to talk first.

"Heath?" Garrett asked, glancing up from his computer tablet. The cargo was almost down.

"You planning to do your head count, Lieutenant?" the Marine veteran asked. "I figure Chief MacElreath is probably waiting to hear from us."

Garrett winced. He was supposed to have confirmed that everyone on the strike team had made the jump successfully and safely. He should have done it before he'd radioed for the cargo drop.

Now he wasn't sure what to do. Finish monitoring the cargo drop that he'd already called for? Pass the tablet off to Sergeant Rodgers? Delegate the head count to Rodgers?

"Um . . ." Garrett hesitated. "I got ahead of myself, Rodgers. Do you think you could —"

"Already did," Rodgers said, furling his brow. "Count's good. All jumpers accounted for. No injuries. Want me to call it in?"

Lieutenant Garrett considered letting him, but it wasn't exactly protocol. The next person up in the chain of authority would be expecting to hear from the strike team leader, not one of the random crew bosses from the team.

"I'll take care of it," he said. "For now, I want you to round everybody up on this hill so we can set up camp, and I can hand out assignments."

"Shouldn't we get the gear first?" Rodgers asked, nodding toward Garrett's tablet. "We might need that to make camp."

Lieutenant Garrett felt his ears redden. *What am I thinking? Of course we need the gear first*, he thought.

Sergeant Rodgers's gaze was making him nervous. The Marine wasn't scowling at him, exactly, but he looked like he was trying very hard not to. It occurred to Garrett that Sergeant Rodgers had several years of wildland firefighting under his belt. Lieutenant Garrett — with none to speak of — wasn't making a great impression of his alleged leadership skills.

"Right, right," he said. "Tell you what, round up your crew, Rodgers. Gather the gear up where it's touched down and bring it here. We'll set up on this hilltop and go from there."

Rodgers's almost-scowl deepened a little into an honest frown. "Wouldn't it make more sense for us to go to where the gear is and set up camp near there? That's assuming it's not closer to the fire than we are, of course."

"Yeah, no, it isn't," Lieutenant Garrett confirmed, feeling more foolish with every word. He checked his high-tech computer tablet again, seeing that the cargo had touched down about a hundred yards behind them. "No, it's farther out. That's a good idea. Let's do that."

"All right," Sergeant Rodgers said. The sour look on his face didn't go away. "I'll start rounding people up." He walked away, calling to his crew and to the other firefighters nearby.

Lieutenant Garrett descended the hill behind him with the tablet in hand. "That could've gone better," he mumbled.

A guy like Sergeant Heath Rodgers was used to the disciplined command and competent professionalism of the Marine Corps. Lieutenant Garrett, thus far, hadn't made a great showing of either. If he kept this up, the lieutenant feared, he'd only be proving right the misgivings some of the experienced firefighters had about him.

But looking like a rookie for a moment wasn't quite as bad as the consequences of failing — namely, losing control of this wildfire.

Lieutenant Garrett needed to prove that he could get the job done. He needed to prove that he deserved to be in charge.

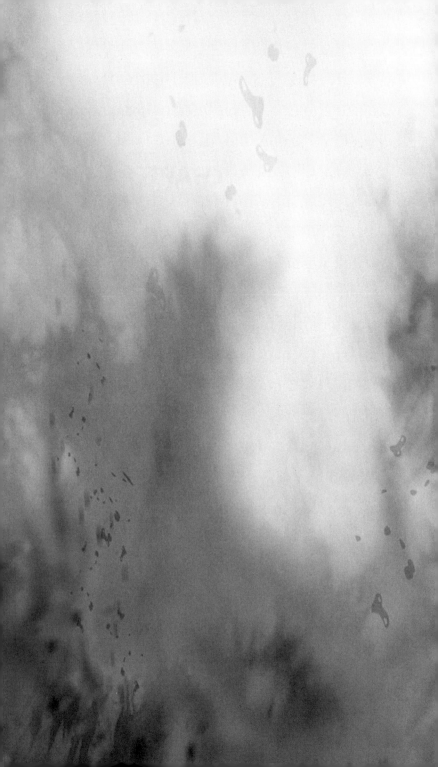

CHAPTER THREE

"Yes, Chief, I guarantee it," Lieutenant Garrett said. Then he switched off his two-way radio.

He'd just guaranteed Chief Anna MacElreath a zero-casualty mission and immediately regretted it. He knew — and he knew that she knew — that there were no guarantees in wildfire fighting.

"Rookie mistake," Lieutenant Garrett said to himself.

Then he shook off the statement and gathered his strike team around the spot where the cargo bundles had landed. Then he turned to his crew bosses. "Break down the crates," Lieutenant Garrett commanded. "Start distributing the crews' gear."

Most of the gear in the cargo drop was camping supplies of one variety or another: tents, bedrolls, water, a generator, a folding camp stove, electric lanterns, toilet paper. Basically everything the team would need to weather a night in the wild.

The crates included eight heavy-duty chain saws, as well as drip-torches and all the gas and oil required to operate them. Each team was issued a pump-operated, shoulder-mounted bladder bag capable of carrying five gallons of water.

The last bit packed down on the final pallet was a bundle of replacement handles for the hand axes, shovels, fire rakes, and other hand tools the team would employ on the fire lines.

The Firestormers had jumped with a full kit of personal work and protective gear as well. Their uniforms were simpler than the bunker gear Lieutenant Garrett was used to wearing into a burning building. Bunker gear consisted of heavy boots, a thick jacket and pants, an air tank, a respirator mask, and the traditional "metro" style fire helmet.

Working long hours outdoors would've been impossible in such heavy clothing, however, so wildland firefighters preferred simpler, lighter garb. They wore lightweight Nomex shirts and tear- and fire-resistant cargo pants. Their boots were heavy-duty logging boots of tough leather with chain-saw-cut-resistant steel caps in the toes. On their heads they wore basic construction-style hard hats.

Already the crew had dumped their chute riggings and cargo webbing with which they had carried their individual gear. The less they took with them to the fire line, the longer they'd be able to work before exhaustion set in.

As for the gear they would be carrying, it was all surprisingly low-tech. The systems in place to guide the firefighting effort were state of the art, but the means of actually fighting the fire were quite the opposite. The Firestormers' main weapons against the blaze were chain saws for clearing trees and hand tools, such as Pulaski axes, shovels, and sturdy fire rakes.

Also among the Firestormers' kit were several bottles of water and a single plastic-wrapped meal of high-energy, high-salt food for lunch. These military-style rations were called "meals, ready to eat" or MREs.

Lastly, each firefighter carried a first aid kit and an emergency fire shelter. Nobody looked forward to a situation that required them to use those two things.

While the crew bosses distributed the gear, Lieutenant Garrett and the strike team rangers set camp as quickly as they could. The remote command center would serve as the lieutenant's base of operations while he coordinated with Chief MacElreath at Incident Command.

The remote command center was where he'd call the team back for dinner. It was where everyone would sleep if their efforts required them to stay in the field for more than a day.

Once the basic structure of the camp was in place, Lieutenant Garrett called his crew bosses, their crews, and his rangers together at the center.

Garrett plugged his high-tech tablet into a small, portable projector.

At once, the image from his tablet leaped onto the tent's canvas wall. The image showed a satellite photo of the forest before the fire.

"Well, here we are," Lieutenant Garrett told his Firestormers. "Beautiful and scenic Klamath National Forest, not too many miles from the Oregon border."

Wavy contour lines covered the topographical map like a giant fingerprint. Steep hills and thickly wooded terrain dominated the geography.

The nearest residents were miles from this command post and roads didn't stretch out this far into the wild. That was why the strike team parachuted in rather than driving or walking.

If the fire had been burning close to a usable road, Incident Command could have deployed engines and water tenders, or even bulldozers to manage the landscape and contain the flames. If the fire had been slightly farther from the roads but over less steep and awful terrain, Garret's strike team could have driven by buggy and then carried their gear on foot like a typical Hotshot crew.

While recruiting the Firestormers, Chief MacElreath insisted that its members cross-train as both Hotshots and smokejumpers. That way, they could deploy where they were needed most.

This time, the conditions called for a strategic airdrop.

"Anyway," Lieutenant Garrett went on, "let's map out our fire. Our best estimates judging from local weather patterns suggest the fire started from multiple lightning strikes, right around here." The lieutenant pointed to a red, flashing dot on the projected image. "Six o'clock last night is when the calls started coming in to local fire stations about the smoke people could see from their homes."

Decades ago, the Forest Service relied on forest rangers stationed in watchtowers to keep an eye out for smoke from wildfires.

These days, however, budget cuts had stripped those towers of their workers. But at the same time, cell phones and social media widened the net of watchful eyes, especially on the borders of the wildlands.

By the time a fire got big enough to pose any danger to the surrounding forest, it threw up enough smoke and ash for someone to notice and call in. Whether that someone was a resident at the edge of the forest or a hiker on a trail, they got word to local departments, which let the Forestry Service know what was happening.

And now, the evolving procedure was to let Chief MacElreath know, so she could get the Firestormers in on the action.

"Before convection forces got involved," Garrett continued, "the wind was blowing southwest steadily enough to push the fire east-northeast. By the time we got eyes on it and were able to map it, the fire had spread out like this."

Lieutenant Garrett pressed an icon on his tablet and updated the projected map. The highlighted area covered more than a thousand acres. Steady winds and ample fuel allowed the fire to spread over the terrain in an even pattern.

From the point of origin, the inferno spread east-northeast in a bulging, teardrop shape. No wildfire burned so evenly for long, however, especially over such hilly and uneven terrain.

Fire typically flowed over a landscape like water — not downhill, exactly, but seeking out paths of least resistance. In fact, the path of least resistance for a fire usually meant an uphill climb. Usually, but not always.

Garrett pressed another icon on his high-tech tablet.

"And this is our most recent report," he said as the map changed again.

The image that took its place looked like an oak leaf. All around the perimeter of the fire front, individual tendrils of flame reached out from the main body like fingers spreading out from a hand.

The Firestormers looked on in silence, now knowing the severity of the blaze.

"These are what we're here to fight," Lieutenant Garrett said, trying to pump up his crews. "If we cut off these fingers of the fire, we can contain this blaze and let it burn itself out before it puts any lives or property in danger."

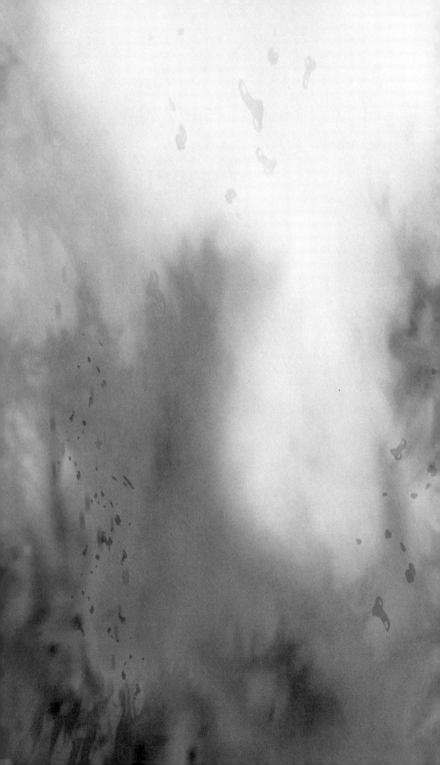

CHAPTER FOUR

Lieutenant Garrett looked away from the projector screen, hoping to see two dozen inspired faces ready to get to work. Instead, he saw a bunch of bored men and women staring at him impatiently.

"Is this going to take long, Lieutenant?" Rodgers asked. "There's still some forest left."

A few firefighters chuckled at that. All of them were from Rodgers's crew. Most of the other firefighters hid their amusement. One of his other crew bosses, Chris Richards, ignored the comment altogether. The third,

Michael Raphael, rolled his eyes. The last, Sergeant Amalia Rendon, frowned and cast a disapproving glance at Rodgers.

"Right, right," Lieutenant Garrett said. He tried not to let the comment rattle him, but he could feel his ears redden again. "Anyway, these are the deployment points around the fire. All strike teams should be in position now."

After another couple of taps on his tablet, a handful of green dots appeared at evenly spaced points around the fire's perimeter. Each one marked a strike team deployed on Chief MacElreath's orders to a point of attack near the largest fingers of the fire.

"This is us," Lieutenant Garrett continued, tapping one of the dots.

The other green dots represented local firefighters deployed from their own stations to contain isolated fires nearby. None of them, Garrett noticed, were as deep in the wilderness or as close to the ever-moving fire front as the Firestormers.

"Our job's simple," he said. "We're going to lock down the fingers of this fire as quickly as possible. Chief MacElreath is counting on us to keep the fire from spreading to the isolated fires that the locals have almost contained."

"Any idea who's working the isolated fires?" Sergeant Rodgers interrupted.

The question caught Garrett off guard. "Huh? Um, I'm not . . ." He tapped his tablet a few times and scratched his head. "No, it doesn't say here. Why?"

"If we're going to be watching their backs, we should know if we can rely on them to be watching ours," Rodgers explained.

Lieutenant Garrett frowned in frustration. "Well, judging by the terrain it'll have to be a Hotshot crew. The fire's too far off roads for dozers, engines, or tenders. They're locals so they know the area. They managed eighty-percent containment of the isolated fires, so they're pretty good. Add that to the fact that Chief MacElreath let them stay where they are after she decided where to send us. I guess if you trust the chief's judgment, you can safely assume this Hotshot crew's going to be just fine watching your back. Any more questions?"

The Firestormers looked on silently.

"Okay then," said Garrett, wrapping up his pregame speech. "Let's get this done."

Lieutenant Garrett had expected those words to sound more stirring than they had.

Maybe I should quit wasting time pumping these people up and just get on with the details, he thought.

After all, this work probably seemed more commonplace for them than it did for him. This was his first wildfire — his first command. He was the only one out here with something to prove. Everyone else was just doing their job. They didn't need inspiration. They were all professionals.

Lieutenant Garrett found himself gritting his teeth. He was embarrassing himself.

Fortunately, Sergeant Amalia Rendon came to his aid. With no trace of judgment or boredom or disappointment on her face, she stepped forward and cleared her throat to get Garrett's attention.

"Sounds good, Lieutenant," she said. She gave him a reassuring, respectful nod. "Where's the anchor, and what's the plan?"

Lieutenant Garrett took a deep breath and let his mind shift gears. It was the sort of question he'd been trained to think through.

When he spoke earlier with Chief MacElreath, she had suggested where the strike teams might anchor their fire lines. But rather than giving Garrett a direct assignment of where to start, she'd encouraged the lieutenant to review the maps and aerial photos for himself.

"All right," Lieutenant Garrett said, isolating and enlarging a section of the map on his tablet. "As you can see here, there's a rocky canyon due south. That'll make a perfect natural firebreak. We'll start our line there and cut east-northeast up to Strike Two's anchor at the quarry."

He shrunk the map back down and used a stylus to draw a rough line from point to point. Rather than drawing a straight line, he traced the topography as best he could to most accurately represent the path his team would take.

"That line's about a mile longer than it needs to be," Rodgers piped up, unasked.

"You've got it anchored behind the wind, and its tail edge curves out too far from the fire front before it joins up with Strike Two. It's inefficient, at best."

"Scared of a little extra hard work, Heath?" Sergeant Rendon said, smirking at him in a not-unfriendly way.

Sergeant Rodgers took her ribbing, but it didn't change his distaste for the lieutenant's proposed fire line. "Hard work's one thing, Amalia," he said, "but you know what kind of time frame we're dealing with. This kid's giving up acres of forest, and he's going to grind us into the ground trying to get this line dug on Chief MacElreath's schedule."

Lieutenant Garrett ground his teeth now. It was bad enough making himself look like a rookie with an less than inspirational speech. He didn't need Rodgers actively undermining his authority on top of that.

"Hey," he snapped, putting a gravelly edge in his voice. Silence fell. Rodgers actually flinched at the interruption. "That's 'Lieutenant This Kid' to you, Heath."

Lieutenant Garrett locked eyes with Rodgers and then grinned to stick a pin in the bubble of tension. Everyone relaxed. A few of the veterans chuckled and nodded approvingly at the lieutenant. Rendon gave a surprised snort of laughter.

"Fair enough," Rodgers said, backing down. "But do you at least see my point about the line?"

"This fire's moving and growing fast," Lieutenant Garrett said, "and the winds are unpredictable. If they shift and push this finger backward, I want it running up against that canyon and stopping. If we leave a gap back there and it gets in behind us, it's almost all uphill to this spot we're standing on."

This drew a few murmurs from the firefighters. Wildfires moved faster uphill than downhill. A fast-moving flame behind them — however unlikely — would have been a serious problem.

"As for the tail end," Lieutenant Garrett continued, "yeah, that balloons out a bit. At the fire's current growth rate, it's not going to be anywhere near that by the time we link up to Strike Two's anchor. But you know better than I do how unpredictable fire is. If the fire front starts running before we get near that quarry, you're going to be glad for the extra distance between you and it."

Sergeant Rodgers frowned thoughtfully but offered no further protest to Lieutenant Garrett's command. More importantly, the other firefighters and crew bosses were nodding along, seeing the sense in the lieutenant's cautious line.

"As far as the plan of attack goes," Lieutenant Garrett said, breathing a little easier, "we'll keep it simple since this is our first time out. We'll do a bump-and-jump, short legs, maximum twelve-hour shifts."

Heads nodded all around, taking in the information.

"All right, class dismissed," Garrett joked, winning polite chuckles. "Crews, get your gear ready. Make sure you have everything you need. Rangers and crew bosses stick around. I'll give you your specifics."

The majority of the Firestormers backed off to perform one last check of their gear before setting out. The crew bosses and the strike team's complement of four rangers closed in around Lieutenant Garrett and waited.

"Does anybody want to admit they have the slowest crew?" the lieutenant asked them.

"If you're trying to figure out line order," Rodgers said, "my guys will take the far end. We're all military —" He paused there, and a shadow of some unpleasant thought drifted across his expression. "Former military, that is. The walk out to the end and the long walk back after hours will be easiest on us."

"Sounds good to me," Lieutenant Garrett said with a shrug. He pointed to one of the rangers, who nodded. "You're with Calvin Walker."

"Where do we start?" the ranger asked.

To answer, Lieutenant Garrett called up another map on his tablet. This one traced his proposed fire line but divided it into equal segments, or legs. The lieutenant focused the map on the first four legs of the fire line.

He tapped the point at the head of the fourth leg. Its map coordinates and its GPS coordinates popped up next to it.

"Here," Garrett said. "Topography says it's on a hilltop but visibility won't be great until you start your line. Ready for coordinates?"

The men both nodded.

Sergeant Rodgers and the ranger each held up a hand. On his forearm, Rodgers wore a snug Nomex bracer that held a smartphone-sized tablet similar to the lieutenant's. Each of the Firestormers' crew bosses had one. The devices allowed Garrett to send them select information from his tablet, keeping everyone informed about the advance of the fire.

The rangers wore smart watches instead of the bracers. The watches connected wirelessly to high-tech glasses. Each pair of glasses included a tiny camera mounted next to the wearer's temple and a tiny speaker built into the earpiece. Next to the camera, a crystal-clear prism extended over the lens of the sunglasses, just outside the wearer's field of view. A microscopic, projector could display images into that prism, such as maps and weather data, for the rangers to review on site.

"Ready," Rodgers said, holding up his bracer. Walker, the ranger, nodded as well.

Lieutenant Garrett double clicked the coordinates he'd called up. He aimed his computer tablet in the two men's direction and swiped the image toward them. Rodgers's bracer and Walker's smart watch beeped.

"Got it," Walker said. Rodgers nodded.

"We'll take the anchor leg," Sergeant Rendon said. "My crew is pretty quick. We'll keep the line bumping along."

"We'll take leg two." Richards said. To Rendon, he grinned and said, "Catch us if you can, Miss Molly." Rendon jokingly elbowed him in the ribs.

"That leaves you on leg three, Angel," Sergeant Rendon said to Michael Raphael, the last crew boss. "Good luck ever getting a leg done."

"Less work for my team," Raphael said, feigning a careless shrug. "And don't call me Angel."

Lieutenant Garrett assigned a ranger to each crew and swiped them each a set of coordinates for where to begin. When they were all ready to go, he said, "Look, let's keep it careful and routine out there, okay?"

"We'll make sure you stay nice and bored," Sergeant Rendon said with a grin. "Just try not to fall asleep while we're out there doing all the hard work."

The crew bosses and their rangers laughed. Lieutenant Garrett laughed along with them. "No promises," he joked. "Now start walking."

One by one, the crew bosses saluted Lieutenant Garrett — first Rendon and then Richards and Raphael.

Sergeant Rodgers hesitated.

"Is there a problem?" Garrett asked him.

After a moment, Rodgers shook his head, forcefully saluted, and then turned and walked into the forest.

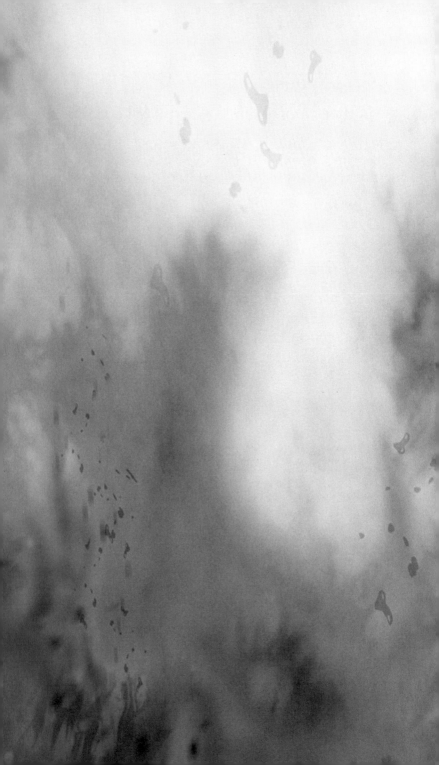

CHAPTER FIVE

When his crew had left, Lieutenant Garrett buried his face in his laptop again. His responsibilities as strike team leader gave him no opportunities to fall asleep, much less get bored. Although he wasn't on the fire line himself, digging firebreaks, it was his responsibility to monitor the progress of his crew and communicate that progress to Incident Command. To that end, he had a few tools at his disposal — some of which he'd never dreamed of needing while working structure fires in the burbs.

The main communication tool was his radio. With a flick of a button, he could switch between three frequencies on which he carried out three different conversations. The main frequency was his channel back to Incident Command. From them, he got big-picture information about the overall spread of the fire, weather conditions, and the availability of supplies and air support.

The second channel connected him to his crew bosses. If they were straying too far from his fire line, he could correct their courses. If they were falling behind schedule, he could urge them to pick up the pace.

The third channel connected Garrett to his rangers. These Firestormers didn't carry hand tools or chain saws. Instead, they carried binoculars, ropes, tree-climbing spurs, maps, and a five-gallon bladder bag of water with a hand-pump sprayer. It was each ranger's job to orbit their crew, scouting the area for dangers. They also developed escape routes should the fire advance faster than they could contain it.

The two-way radio was the lowest-tech part of Garrett's equipment. His tablet was more powerful than his personal computer. It was wrapped in a waterproof, shock-resistant casing. He could drop it down a rocky hill and expect to find it perfectly functional at the bottom. The tablet was the heart of Garrett's capabilities in the field, as well as his lifeline back to Incident Command in an emergency.

Without it, he'd be blind to ongoing fire and weather conditions. He'd have to rely on hand drawing lines on paper maps as his crews and rangers reported their status. It could be done — it *had been* done for decades — but the tablet made everything so much easier.

Yet, despite the sci-fi level technology, everything came down to the sweat and toil of Firestormers on the front lines. Lieutenant Garrett could direct their efforts and watch over them remotely, but it was up to them to get the job done. And if there was anything his brief, intensive field training had taught him, it was that that job *sucked*.

Lieutenant Garrett knew the basic strategy of fighting a wildfire was simple enough. Map out the total area of the fire. Then surround it with non-flammable firebreaks, so the blaze couldn't grow any larger.

When the area was accessible by roads, bulldozers could cut those firebreaks. In this case, however, that wasn't an option. That left the work to Firestormers, who set to it with strength and obsessive determination. Their job was to clear lines that were miles long and dozens of feet wide of everything from trees to brush to grass. They'd clear-cut the area and dig it down to the soil, so that nothing left would burn.

Each five-person crew boasted two sawyers, armed with gasoline-powered chain saws. They were responsible for bringing down trees along the fire line and cutting them into manageable chunks.

Moving behind them was the swamper, whose job it was to drag those chunks off the fire line. The swamper also carried the extra gas, oil, and tools to keep the sawyers' saws working.

The rest of the crew followed with hand tools doing the hottest, nastiest, dirtiest work. With hard, sharp shovels, Pulaski fire axes, and steel fire rakes, they uprooted undergrowth and broke up the underlying dirt until nothing remained. They called themselves grunts, because by the end of a backbreaking shift, they were barely capable of speaking more than that.

At camp, Garrett sweltered in the California heat, and he didn't have a hundred-foot wall of fire to contend with. He could hear the roar of the distant blaze, and it set his instincts on edge. He felt guilty. Garrett knew he was capable of doing the work his crews were doing — he wouldn't have made it into the Firestormers program otherwise — but he preferred the demands that being in charge thrust on him instead.

As the day went on, Lieutenant Garrett couldn't help wonder if that preference meant he wasn't truly Firestormers material. If he'd made it onto the team as a grunt rather than riding his father's influence to the rank of lieutenant, could he hack it on the line? Could he do the work and keep up good spirits the way Sergeant Rendon seemed able to do? Could he attack the problem with endless gung-ho determination like Sergeant Rodgers?

He didn't know, and not knowing bothered him.

If he was asking these men and women to follow his lead, they needed to feel like he was one of them. They needed to know they could count on him. They needed to know they could trust him, as they trusted one another.

Just then, Lieutenant Garrett received an incoming call on this two-way radio. "Go ahead, Chief?" He prompted Anna MacElreath, awaiting her hourly updates from Incident Command.

"Yep . . . Got it . . . Yep . . . The bird? . . . Oh . . . Really?" Garrett listened and responded as the chief rattled off a list of questions and updates. "Rodgers? Yes, ma'am, he's on the

fire line with his crew . . . Oh . . . Okay . . . Yep,
I'll make sure he gets the message."

Lieutenant Garrett switched off the radio.
The first day on a big fire is always the worst, he
thought.

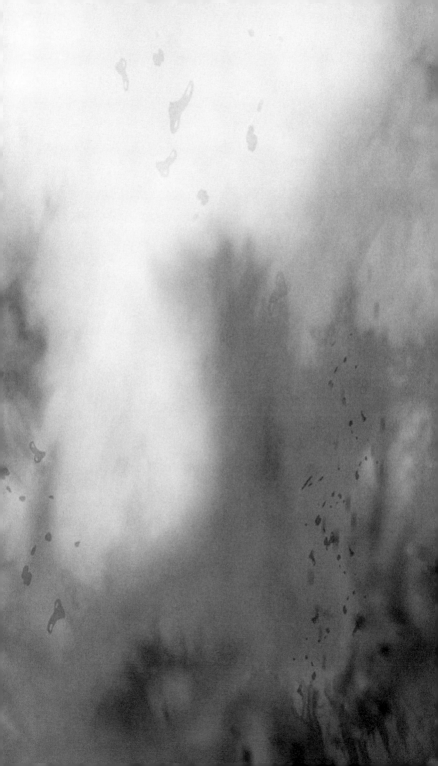

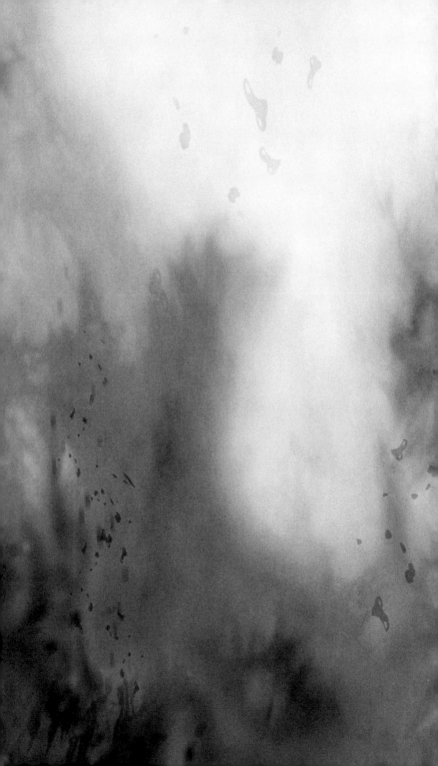

CHAPTER SIX

Lieutenant Garrett sighed. "Time to get back to work," he told himself, burying his face in his tablet.

What was supposed to be an eight-hour shift on the line for the Firestormers turned into thirteen, fourteen, and then fifteen.

Lieutenant Garrett monitored that effort on his tablet, marveling at the speed with which his plan came together. All of the strike teams made rapid progress, digging their firebreaks without any casualties or wasted efforts. Each team — from elite Firestormers to the local firefighters — traced out its lines perfectly.

They quickly achieved containment around the fire faster than it could advance.

The Firestormers were by far the fastest workers on the blaze. Sergeant Rendon's crew members were the quickest on the line, and Sergeant Rodgers's were undoubtedly the toughest. That latter quality turned out to be what was most important as day turned to night.

By the end of the hour sixteen, Garrett was ready to call his teams for their evening meal — to be airdropped presently — and a well-deserved sleep shift. Containment efforts were going so well, however, that Chief MacElreath didn't want to slow the pace and potentially give up the advantage.

Judging wind and weather patterns, Incident Command called for another three hours on shift to try to sew up the perimeter.

Lieutenant Garrett's crew bosses had each laughed at him over the radio when he'd relayed that information and tried to apologize to them for it. They'd apparently seen the extension coming before the lieutenant had.

When the seventeen-hour mark rolled around and Incident Command had called for another extension, however, the crew bosses' reaction was restrained. Grim even.

Their crews had long since eaten their MREs and the energy bars they'd brought along as between-meal snacks. Everyone had been back at least once for more water, and the early afternoon's mad rush of progress along the fire line had slowed to a crawl.

The fire was bearing down on the crews along all sides of the fire front, but the containment perimeter was *almost* finished, so Chief MacElreath made the call to keep the crews in place until the job was done. It hadn't been what the weary firefighters wanted to hear, but the crew bosses agreed that it was probably the right call.

The official end of their day came around two o'clock the next morning.

One by one, his crew bosses reported in that they'd finished their legs and Richards's and Raphael's crews had already met up at the abandoned quarry.

Lieutenant Garrett reported that information back to Incident Command, but he was so strung out from the day spent coordinating and communicating back and forth that he didn't realize the significance of that development at first. It wasn't until Chief MacElreath got on the radio herself and congratulated him on his job that

Lieutenant Garrett realized the job was actually getting done.

The fire wasn't out — there were still days of work yet to do — but it was nearing containment. No one had lost their lives yet. No property had been destroyed. The Firestormers' mission was, by all accounts, turning out to be a success.

Only one question remained, and Sergeant Rodgers asked it while he had Lieutenant Garrett on the radio.

"I need permission to backburn this area, Lieutenant," Rodgers told him. "I've got a missing man out here somewhere, and I need more time. A backburn could drive the fire away from here."

Lieutenant Garrett shook his head and relayed what Incident Command had told him earlier. "Negative. The wind's not right on our side. Strike Two and Strike Three's lines are upwind, though. They're going to backburn on their side, and the wind should push it around toward us before our finger gets here."

"Yes or no would have been fine," Sergeant Rodgers sighed.

"Fair enough," Garrett said, knowing he didn't have to hold Rodgers's hand like that. "That's a negative. Now get out of there before it's too late. We'll send another team of search-and-rescue choppers after your man. It's too dangerous to be in there on foot."

The two-way radio began to crackle, and Lieutenant Garrett fiddled with its channel. Then, after a moment, Rodgers's broken voice came through. "Negative," the sergeant responded.

The radio crackled again. "Rodgers," Garrett said into it, "that wasn't a suggestion. That was an order." The lieutenant released the radio's Call switch, but only but static came back at him.

"Rodgers!" he shouted into the device. "Rodgers! Get out of there!"

Nothing but static.

CHAPTER SEVEN

Lieutenant Garrett passed the news on to the other bosses and then let Incident Command know his people were on the way back. It actually took him another moment to remember that his rangers weren't in direct contact with the bosses by radio. Raphael's and Richards's rangers were already with their respective crew bosses, but Rodgers' ranger, Walker, was still in the field.

Rodgers's radio wasn't responding, but maybe Walker's communicator was still functional. When he reached Walker, Garrett realized he had a problem. Rodgers and Walker weren't together.

At the same time, Rendon's team was just returning, dragging their tools behind them and shambling like the walking wounded. Lieutenant Garrett directed them to the feast that Incident Command had airdropped.

As they started eating, Lieutenant Garrett checked his tablet to monitor the other crews' progress back to camp. He got good readings from the GPS transponders in his crew bosses' datapads and the rangers' smart watches, but what those readings told him was troubling. Sergeant Rodgers was still where he had been when Garrett lost contact.

"What is it?" Sergeant Rendon asked, noticing Garrett's expression. She drifted over to him with a foil-wrapped hoagie in each hand. One of them already open and half eaten. Before the lieutenant could answer her, she let out a thunderous belch and leaned back into the sandwich like a starving woman.

"Rodgers is lollygagging," Lieutenant Garrett said, trying to ignore the heavy stench of onions on Rendon's breath.

"He doesn't strike me as the lollygagging type," Rendon pointed out around another bite. Her first hoagie was almost gone already.

"Me either," he agreed. "Something's wrong. Is Edwards still awake?"

Rendon glanced over her shoulder to where the Ranger Edwards was sitting. He had arrived back at camp earlier, with Peter Stoyko and his community in tow. Edwards was chatting them up and feeding them, making them feel comfortable for the moment. As he did, Edwards sucked down egg drop soup from a Styrofoam cup, his first meal in more than twelve hours.

"For the moment," she said.

Lieutenant Garrett's frown deepened. "Tell him to refill his bladder bag and bring it to me."

Rendon didn't question. Finishing off the last bite of her first hoagie and tearing into the foil around the second, she walked over to do as Garrett had asked. Edwards got up, tossed his empty cup in the camp trash bin and retrieved his bladder bag from where he'd stowed it.

Meanwhile, Lieutenant Garrett called Rodgers again on the radio. There was no answer. His worry mounting, he called Walker again.

"Sir?" Walker responded.

"Tell me Rodgers has linked up with you," Lieutenant Garrett prompted.

Walker's reply was much more awake — and alarmed. "That's a negative. We're still waiting for him. Is he having trouble with that spot fire?"

"I called him off. Now he's not responding."

Now Walker's voice was flat, calm, controlled. "Tell me where. We'll go check on him."

"No," Lieutenant Garrett said. "Sit tight."

Sergeant Rendon returned with her ranger's refilled bladder bag on one shoulder just as Walker was replying in protest.

"I caught the last part of that," she said. "Heath's missing?"

Lieutenant Garrett nodded. "He went after a missing man. Alone."

Rendon shook her head and then hefted the ranger's bladder bag on her shoulder. "Is that why you want this? Are you planning to go down the line and look for him?"

"I am."

"Lieutenant, we can't just sit tight with

a man missing," Walker said over the radio. "You can't expect us —"

"Negative!" Lieutenant Garrett snapped back over the channel. "You guys are sleep-deprived and worn down to the bone. I'm not letting you go stumbling over the line in the dark with that fire bearing down on you. Your orders are to wait right there. You read me?"

It took a few long, tense seconds before Walker finally said, "I read you."

"Good. Now stay put and await further orders."

"That's the right call," Rendon said as Garrett reached for the shoulder strap of the bladder bag. She gave it to him reluctantly. "But are you seriously planning to go out there on your own?"

"I am," the lieutenant said again. "I've still got Rodgers's GPS on my tablet. I can go right to him faster than I can talk Walker's team to his position and wait for them to look around in the dark."

"It's miles down that line," Rendon said. "And I know you're tired."

"I've still got some gas in the tank," Garrett said, swallowing a yawn that threatened to undermine his point. He shrugged into the bladder bag and fumbled with resizing the straps. "Besides, I'm not as wiped as you are."

"That leg of the line is out ahead of the front," Rendon said, "but the fire's been picking up speed. By the time you run down to where Rodgers is, the blaze is going to be on top of you. You're not going to have any time even if you know exactly where to go."

"Sure," Garrett told her, "but I'm a firefighter. Danger's part of the job. Besides, what if Rodgers is hurt out there? I'm the only one who knows exactly where he is. He's counting on me."

"We're all counting on you," Rendon said. "We have been all day — but counting on you to keep your wits and think like a leader. Before you go rushing off into the dark like you just told Walker not to do, ask yourself if that's what's best for Rodgers. If he is hurt and does need help, is your running off on foot the best way to get it to him?"

Before Rendon even finished speaking, Lieutenant Garrett had realized she was right. He wasn't thinking; he was letting himself get wrapped up in the moment. He was getting stars in his eyes, seeing this as his big opportunity to prove himself worthy of his Firestormers' respect once and for all.

But that wasn't his job.

"You're right," he said. "That wouldn't help. This will . . ." He switched channels on his radio back to Incident Command. "Command," he said, "I've got a crew boss down in the field, inside the fire line. His transponder's not moving, and he isn't responding to his radio. I need additional air search-and-rescue units. Now."

"You got it," the captain in charge of the Operations Section said. There was a brief pause, and then he added, "Choppers are already in the air. Shoot me your guy's GPS."

Lieutenant Garrett handed Rendon his radio, held up his datapad and sent Rodgers's GPS coordinates and transponder frequency information up the chain of communication. The captain, the lieutenant knew, would pass it over to the chief of his Air Ops branch, who would relay it to the search-and-rescue helicopter pilots.

Garrett took the radio back from Rendon. "Okay, they know where he is," he told her. "Now we just have to wait."

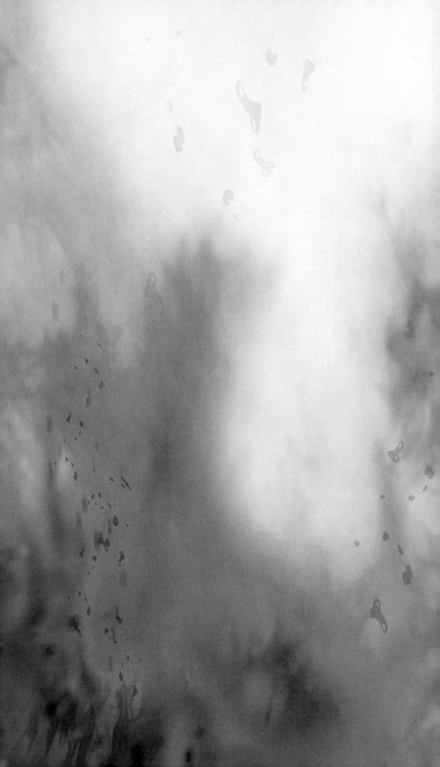

CHAPTER EIGHT

Lieutenant Garrett thought about the guarantee he'd given Chief MacElreath as her voice came over the two-way radio. *Zero casualties.*

That possibility was looking less likely each passing minute.

"We got him, Garrett," Chief MacElreath said without hesitation.

Lieutenant Garrett let out an unexpected sigh of relief.

"Garrett, do you read?" the chief asked after a moment of silence.

"Oh, yes!" the lieutenant exclaimed. "We read you loud and clear!" He smiled at Sergeant Rendon, standing nearby.

"Are all the rest of the Firestormers in?" asked Chief MacElreath. "You didn't send them out to fetch Rodgers, did you?"

"No, ma'am. Just the opposite."

"Good, good. I know Rendon's got more sense, but any of those other knuckleheads would be chomping at the bit to go blundering off in the dark."

Sergeant Rendon grinned at that. The praise seemed to make hours of fatigue melt away, if only for a moment.

"I'll get the chopper pilot on your crew frequency when he's nearing your camp," MacElreath said. "In the meantime, make sure everybody eats, and when the locusts are done, get everybody tucked in. They've earned a rest. That's a good job out there."

"Thank you, ma'am," Garrett said, though Chief MacElreath had already cut the connection and couldn't hear him. He realized when he looked up at Rendon that he was grinning just as wide as she was.

"Feels good, right?" she asked.

"Sure does," he said.

Lieutenant Garrett took a deep breath and then cut the connection and checked his tablet to make sure that Rodgers's GPS transponder was actually moving back toward camp.

It was.

Just then, another call came over the two-way. It was one of the search-and-rescue choppers that Lieutenant Garrett could already hear thumping in the distance.

"Thanks for the ride," Sergeant Rodgers said on the other end.

"You're going to have to thank more

people than me," the lieutenant told him.

Rodgers grunted. "Ha. Thank the system, right?" He hesitated and then, "But you're the one at the controls. And you deserve to be."

"When I talk sense, people listen," Lieutenant Garrett said, finally knowing what it felt like to mean that.

"*When* you talk sense," Rodgers replied, and couldn't help add, "And that ain't often."

"Okay, wise guy, reel in," Garrett told him. "Your dinner's getting cold."

"Yes, sir — I mean, yes, Lieutenant," Rodgers said, signing off.

"I'd say that went well," Lieutenant Garrett said. He lowered his tablet and walked with Sergeant Rendon back over toward the food that Incident Command's logistics people had airdropped in.

Rendon was already halfway done with her second hoagie.

"Pretty well," Sergeant Rendon agreed around a mouthful of sandwich.

"And thanks, by the way," Garrett added. "For your advice, I mean. It helped."

Rendon shrugged that off. "Eh, you would have come to the same conclusion on your own before you even made it to the line. All I did was save you a few minutes of jogging. "

"Still, thanks. Now that we're done for the day, I don't mind admitting I was a little nervous about all this."

"You don't say." Rendon smiled.

Garrett laughed.

Rendon turned to face Garrett and put one sweaty, sooty and now grease-stained hand on his shoulder. "Oh, and another thing, Lieutenant," she said, "I've got something to tell you, and I think you're really going to want to hear it. Frankly, after the day you've had, I think you *deserve* to hear it. Ready?"

"I guess."

"You put your bladder bag on upside down."

At the look on Garrett's face, Rendon and everyone in earshot all burst out laughing.

They were still laughing when the search-and-rescue unit called in with good news.

And Lieutenant Jason Garrett laughed right along with them.

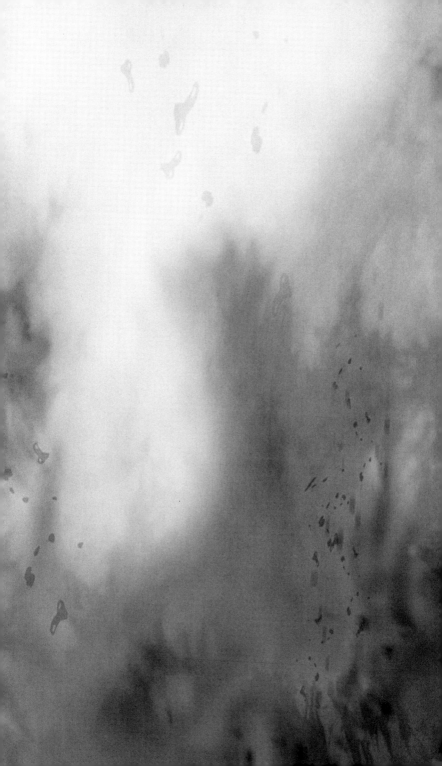

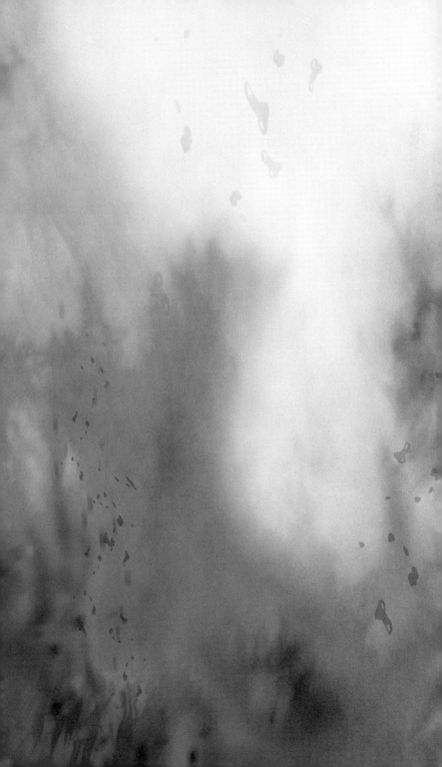

ABOUT THE AUTHOR

Carl Bowen is a father, husband, and writer living in Lawrenceville, Georgia. He has published a handful of novels, short stories, and comics. For Stone Arch Books and Capstone, Carl has retold *20,000 Leagues Under the Sea* (by Jules Verne), *The Strange Case of Dr. Jekyll and Mr. Hyde* (by Robert Louis Stevenson), *The Jungle Book* (by Rudyard Kipling), "Aladdin and His Wonderful Lamp" (from *A Thousand and One Nights*), *Julius Caesar* (by William Shakespeare), and *The Murders in the Rue Morgue* (by Edgar Allan Poe). Carl's novel, *Shadow Squadron: Elite Infantry*, earned a starred review from *Kirkus Book Reviews*.

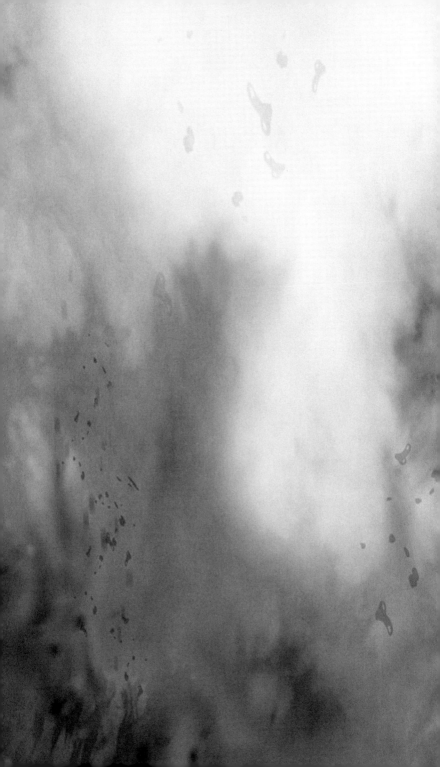

GLOSSARY

adrenaline (uh-DREH-nuh-luhn) — a chemical the body produces when a person is excited

casualty (KAZH-oo-uhl-tee) — someone who is injured, captured, killed, or missing in an accident, a disaster, or a war

Global Positioning System (GLOH-buhl puh-ZI-shuh-ning SISS-tuhm) — an electronic tool used to find the location of an object; this system is often called GPS

inferno (in-FUR-noh) — a very large and dangerous fire

Kevlar (KEV-lahr) — a high-strength material

protocol (PRO-tuh-kahl) — a code of correct behavior usually seen in diplomatic or military services

topographic map (top-uh-GRAF-ik MAP) — a map that shows the heights and positions of a place

FIREFIGHTING EQUIPMENT

PULASKI AXE
A single-bit ax with an adze-shaped
hoe extending from the back.

MCLEOD
A combination hoe and rake used especially
by the U.S. Forest Service in firefighting.

CHAIN SAW
A tool that cuts wood with a circular chain that is driven
by a motor and made up of many connected sharp metal
teeth. Sawyers use chain saws to fell trees on the fire line.

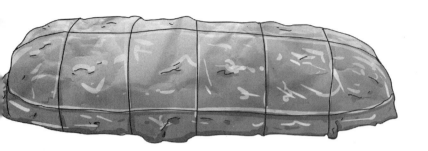

FIRE SHELTER

A small, aluminized tent offering protection in an emergency. The shelter reflects radiant heat and provides breathable air if a firefighter becomes trapped within a blaze.

DRIPTORCH

A handheld canister containing flammable fuel. When ignited, firefighters use driptorches to "drip" flames onto the ground for a controlled burn.

TWO-WAY RADIO

A small radio for receiving and sending messages.

WILDFIRE FACTS

Nearly 90% of wildfires are started by humans. Most of these fires begin by accidental causes, including careless campfires and poorly discarded cigarettes.

Lightning is the leading cause of natural wildfires. Every day, lightning strikes the Earth more than 100,000 times, and 10–20% of those strikes ignite a fire. However, most lightning fires are small and burn out quickly.

An average of 1.2 million acres of forest burns in the United States every year. In 2015, more than 10 million acres burned, setting a new record. Battling these fires cost $1.7 billion.

In extreme wildfires, flames can tower more than 165 feet in the air and reach temperatures of 2,200 degrees Fahrenheit.

The Great Miramichi Fire is the largest wildfire ever recorded. The blaze burned more than 3 million acres throughout New Brunswick, Canada, and Maine, in October 1825. During the fire, 160 lives were lost.

On June 30, 2013, nineteen members of the Granite City Hotshots were killed during the Yarnell Hill Fire in Yarnell, Arizona. It was the deadliest day for U.S. firefighters since the terrorist attacks on September 11, 2001.

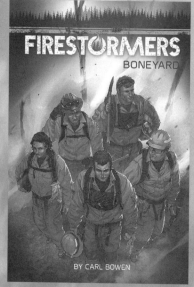

THEN CHECK OUT . . .
SHADOW SQUADRON
ALSO BY CARL BOWEN

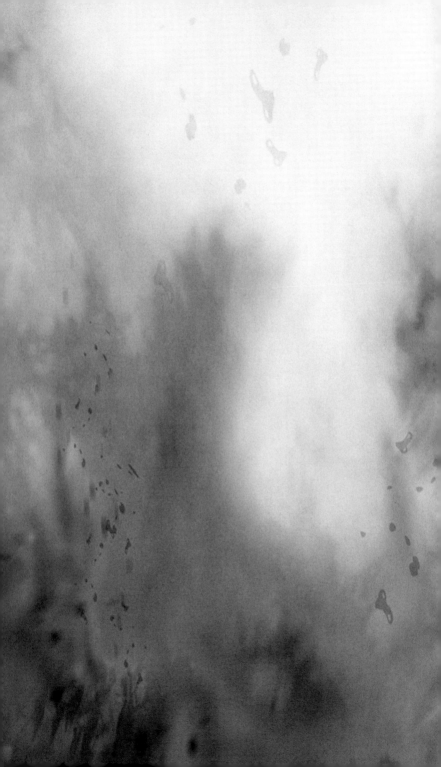